W9-ALN-894

NEVER FORGOTTEN

To my grandsons, John-John, James Everett, Peter, and Mark—P.C.M.

For Anne and Lee, and thanks to Randy and Tina—L.D. & D.D.

Text copyright © 2011 by Patricia C. McKissack
Illustrations copyright © 2011 by Leo and Diane Dillon
All rights reserved. Published in the United States by Schwartz & Wade Books, an imprint of
Random House Children's Books, a division of Random House, Inc., New York.
Schwartz & Wade Books and the colophon are trademarks
of Random House, Inc.
Visit us on the Web! www.randomhouse.com/kids
Educators and librarians, for a variety of teaching tools,
visit us at www.randomhouse.com/teachers
Library of Congress Cataloging-in-Publication Data
McKissack, Pat.
Never Forgotten / Patricia C. McKissack ;
illustrated by Leo and Diane Dillon. p. cm.
Summary: In eighteenth-century West Africa, a boy raised by his blacksmith father and the
Mother Elements—Wind, Fire, Water, and Earth—is captured and taken to America as a slave.

ISBN 978-0-375-84384-6 (trade) — ISBN 978-0-375-94453-6 (glb)
ISBN 978-0-375-98387-0 (ebook)
[1. Novels in verse. 2. Families—Fiction. 3. Slavery—Fiction. 4. Four elements
(Philosophy)—Fiction. 5. Blacksmiths—Fiction. 6. Blacks—Mali—Fiction. 7. African
Americans—Fiction.] I. Dillon, Leo, ill. II. Dillon, Diane, ill. III. Title.
PZ7.5.M45Ne 2011
[Fic]—dc22
2010024789

The text of this book is set in Celestia Antique.
The illustrations were rendered in acrylic and watercolor on bristol board.

MANUFACTURED IN CHINA
10 9 8 7 6 5 4 3 2 1
Random House Children's Books supports the
First Amendment and celebrates the right to read.

NEVER FORGOTTEN

—◁◇▷—

by PATRICIA C. McKISSACK
artwork by LEO & DIANE DILLON

schwartz & wade books · new york

The Griot's Prelude

1725
Old Mali in the Sahel,
West Africa

BEWARE
The drums speak
A single message—a warning:
Beware
Of pale men riding in large seabirds
With great white wings.
Beware
Of men with the blue of the sky in their eyes,
Who steal upriver
Through the Great Forest mists
And into the Savannah Lands in search of slaves—
Us.
Beware!
Hear the moans and groans of their captives—
Hundreds, thousands stolen.
We rarely speak of the Taken,
But I will, just once,
Because you asked.

DINGA, THE BLACKSMITH

Back
   Back
      Back
At the far edge of memory,
We recall a Mende blacksmith,
Dinga—

By all accounts a master craftsman,
An artisan worthy of praise.
Honored as a powerful magician,
One who could speak the old names
Of the Mother Elements,
Earth,
Fire,
Water,
Wind,
And they would do his bidding—
Dinga!
People sang praise songs to him.
Listen.

> "Dog, oh, dog, great among your kind
> Guards man.
> Woman, oh, woman, great among women
> Works hard for your children.
> Hunter, oh, hunter, great among your brethren
> Provides meat for the villagers.
> Warrior, oh, warrior, great among your ranks
> Protects your families.
> King, oh, king, great like no other
> Shares with the people.
> Blacksmith, oh, blacksmith, greatest among us because you serve us all."

Though Dinga was a gifted blacksmith,
First among the first,
He is remembered
Best for being a loving father.

A FATHER'S JOURNEY BEGINS

When Dinga's beloved wife of only a year
Died giving birth,
Dinga put away his sorrow
And embraced his newborn son.
"I will raise you myself,"
He declared.

The elder women of his village
Argued against it, saying,
"He will grow up wild
Without the gentle hand of a mother
To guide him.
You must abide by custom:
Take another wife,
Or give the baby to a woman who is childless."

But Dinga could not be persuaded.

"How will you feed the baby?"
The women argued.
"You have no milk to give."

Still, Dinga would not change his mind.
"The tortoise does not have milk to give
But it knows how to take care of its young,"
He replied.
Then, shamelessly,
He tied the baby on his back
Like a woman
And headed for his forge.

THE MOTHER ELEMENTS

At the place where seven generations
Of his clan had once stood,
Dinga set his feet firmly on the ground
And called to Earth,
"DONGI!
Thank you for yielding up the ore
From your underground storehouse of treasures."

Dinga lit the fire in his forge
And called to Fire,
"NGOM-GBI!
Thank you for making the ore pliable
So that I might shape it."

Dinga filled a calabash from the river
And called to Water,
"DZHE-LO-WA!
Thank you for setting the iron
And making it strong."

Dinga pumped the bellows and Fire rose up again.
He called to Wind,
"FE FE!
Thank you for reviving Fire
And keeping my brow cool in the heat of the day."

Then, lifting his arms in praise,
Dinga cried,
"Come now, elders,
Behold my beloved son!"

THE PRESENTATION

Earth Mother appeared first,
Ageless and forever beautiful.
She kissed the child, then spoke softly.
"Ahh! See how he grabs my finger.
Already he is strong like my mountain sons.
Pum Pum Pa Pum Pum Pa."

Fire Woman leaped into the air
And swirled majestically
In her flaming garment of red.
"He does not fear my blaze—
Clearly a sign
He will be a spirited leader,
Inspiring,
Forceful,
Courageous!
Kiki Karum Kiki Karum Kiki Karum."
And she blew the child a warm kiss
That made him coo.

Water Maiden sang to the boy child
An old, old lullaby:
"A baby has come.
He has come,
And happiness has come.
A boy has come.

He has come,
And laughter has come.
A son has come.
He has come,
And beauty has come."

When the child gurgled in reply,
She tickled his toes and said,
"Even now I can hear music in his voice.
Shum Da Da We Da Shum Da Da We Da."

Suddenly,
Wind Spirit swished in—
Turning and spinning,
Flipping and swooping—
And made the baby squeal happily.

Wind gently embraced him
And whispered in his ear,
"We will dance
Through the
Tall grasses,
You and I,
Forever free.
Swi Swi a Swi Swi a Swi Swi a Swi Wa."

Pum Pum Pa Pum Pum Pa
Kiki Karum Kiki Karum Kiki Karum
Shum Da Da We Da Shum Da Da We Da
Swi Swi a Swi Swi a Swi Swi a Swi Wa

THE NAMING

When Dinga invited the Mother Elements
To help with his son's upbringing,
They agreed.
Then he held the baby
Up to the night sky
And named him.
"*Musafa!*
Only the Universe is Greater!"
With the Mother Elements by his side
Dinga danced late into the night,
Celebrating the new family that had been formed.

MUSAFA

The years passed in a march of seasons.
The boy grew tall and strong
Under the loving eyes of his father
And the protective forces of the Mother Elements,
Who were his teachers,
His counselors,
His friends.

He loved debating an idea with Fire,
Laughing with Water,
Resting in the hollow of Earth's arms
As she gave him the wisdom of the ages:
"Fear is a leopard; Courage renders him toothless.
When the drumbeat changes, you must change the dance.
Learn by reaching back with one hand
While stretching forward with the other.
Kings may come and go, but the family endures forever."

But most of all, Musafa enjoyed
Running freely through the tall grasses
With Wind.
Even the village women had to admit that Dinga
Had done a good job of raising
His child.

BEWARE

Drums. War drums.
Benin against Hausa.
Yoruba against Ashanti.
Mandingo against Wolof.
The foreigners against all.
Bloodshed.
Violence.
Chaos.
The Drums spoke of treachery—
Pumpumpumpum pumpum pum pumpumpum.
Dinga heard the Drums' song,

But it was far away and had nothing to do with him,
So he didn't worry.
He wasn't careful. . . .

MUSAFA BECOMES AN APPRENTICE

In due time
Musafa took his place beside Dinga
As a blacksmith's apprentice.
"You are the eighth generation
Of our clan to wield a hammer,"
Said Dinga proudly.
Musafa wanted to be as good as his father expected,
But no matter how hard he tried, his work was uninspired.
His spear blades were unbalanced,
And his tools were brittle.
Still, he had a knack for shaping scraps of metal
Into exact copies of whatever caught his eye:
A creeping caterpillar, a sleeping crocodile,
A tickbird, a stand of savannah grass.

"Musafa makes pretty things, yes!
But useless!" Dinga complained to the Mother Elements.

"*All he needs is time,*" hissed Fire.
"*Be patient,*" said Earth.
"*One day, his hammer will find a song,*" Water added.

And so Dinga allowed Musafa
To continue hammering out beautifully decorated,
Useless objects.

GONE!

One morning,
Dinga sent Musafa into the bush for brushwood.
It wasn't too far;
It shouldn't have taken too long.
When Musafa did not return,
Dinga thought,
Oh, he must be running with Wind again
Rather than doing his chores.
Then darkness came.
And Dinga grew anxious.
He searched for Musafa in all his favorite places.
Nothing.
"Where are you, boy! Where? Where?"
Dinga asked the Villagers to help search.
He called his child's name again and again.
"Musafa, answer me now! This is no time to tease!"
Fear overtook Dinga, and he cried out.
"My son, if you hear me, please answer."
Searching along the road,
Dinga found a small leather pouch.
He had made it for Musafa,
And the boy would never have parted with it.
Agony!
I should have gathered the wood myself.
I should not have sent him alone.
I should not have . . .
Dinga tore his clothing and
Threw dirt on his head as a sign of great sorrow.

THE SEARCH

In his time of desperation,
Dinga called upon the great Elements.
"Dongi!
Ngom-gbi!
Dzhe-lo-wa!
Fe Fe!
Please find my son."

Earth,
Seated and still,
Sighed deeply.
"*I know Musafa's familiar footfall.
I will go fetch him.*"

When Earth returned sometime later,
Shaken, anguished,
Dinga begged, "Tell me! Did you see him?"
Has my son been trampled by a herd of stampeding elephants?"
"*No! Worse!*"
"Has he been mangled by a lion?"
"*No! Worse!*"
"What terrible news must I endure?"
This is the story Earth told.

Earth's Answer

"MASTER BLACKSMITH, I *saw our beloved boy.*
   Standing on the shoulders of my mountain sons,
   I saw Musafa
   Where the herds run and the lions hunt.

   "*I watched as he was bound to other captives*
   Ankle to ankle.
   I watched as he was force-marched toward the Big Water—
   Tripping, stumbling, falling.
   I watched him take a lash
   Across his bare back so hard
   His body trembled.
   But I saw something else, too—
   Musafa stopping to help
   A girl from a neighboring village.
   He used an old saying I taught him.
   '*Sister, little Sister,' he cried.*
   '*Fear is a leopard; Courage renders him toothless.*
   Gather your courage. Be strong!'
   I shook and tore my garments,
   But I could not drive the captors back."
   (Villagers along the Niger River
   Still tell how earthquakes split the Earth
   And heaved up smoking rock
   The day Musafa was taken.)
   "Yes, *I saw our beloved son.*
   He is one of the Taken.
   But no help, no help, no help could I give.
   Pumpumpumpum pumpum pum pumpumpum."

FIRE FLARES

"*I will force the captors to release Musafa,*"
Said Fire.
She collected her power into a flaming ball,
Then burst out of the forge.
She touched a blade of grass with her fingertip,
And a blazing wall engulfed the grasslands
In pursuit of the intruders.
(Villagers still tell how the savannahs were scorched
By Fire's rage when Musafa was taken.)
"Fire will bring him home!" Dinga said, reassured.

But all his hope dissolved
When she returned empty-handed,
Out of breath,
Sputtering,
Spent.
"Oh, what has happened to my son?"
Dinga wailed.
This is the story Fire told.

FIRE'S ORDEAL

"THIEVES!
Chase,
Run,
I *scorch their path.*
Anger!
I *hurl long spears of fire at their heels.*
Rage!
They escape to the sandy beach.
Blocked,
I *can go no farther.*
Fury!
Beyond wait the ships.
I *watch as they load the captives,*
Musafa among them,
Frightened, yet facing the unknown
Bravely!
I *fling a fireball at the sailors.*
Sparks fly.
Still I *cannot cross the sand to reach our son.*
They take him below.
The ships move away on the water,
Great gliding birds with white wings.
I *see him go.*
Gone,
Gone,
Gone!
Kiki Karum Kiki Karum Kiki Karum."

WATER'S PURSUIT

Now Water stood swirling by the bank of the great river.
"I *will pursue Musafa's ship;*
See where it goes; bring you news."
She spread her arms and
The heavens opened.
A deluge swelled the river higher and
Swept her to the Ocean.
(Whenever the Niger River floods,
Villagers still remember Water's efforts
To rescue Musafa.)

Weeks became months
As Dinga waited for news with a weary but hopeful spirit.
Then one day Water returned.
No song accompanied her.
No joy lit her countenance.

"Tell me what you saw?"
Dinga asked,
Though fearful of the answer.
This is the story Water told.

WATER'S TALE

"A LARGE SEA CREATURE *led me to the Silver Star,*
  A two-hundred-ton brig bound for a western shore.
  Its belly bulged with children snatched
  From Mother Africa's arms.
  They screamed curses in a tangle of languages,
  Prayed to God, Allah, and Oshun.
  Death was the Captain of that ship;
  Suffering, an apt first mate;
  Cruelty, the crew.
  Captives, too many to count, died—
  Some by choice!
  So many perished,
  Sharks followed behind the ship
  In anticipation of a grisly meal.
  Yet I heard a single voice singing above the din.
  It was not a joyful song or a carol of glee,
  But a ballad of defiance.
  It was Musafa.
  'The drumbeat has changed,
  We must change our dance.
  Stop crying.
  Be stubborn.
  Refuse to die!
  Live!'
  And even though many of the fellow captives
  Could not understand his language,
  They were comforted.

"That terrible journey across the Big Water—
The Middle Passage—
Ended in the Caribbean Islands;
I stayed near the docks to hear word of
Musafa's fate.
I heard that the captives were sold
In marketplaces along with cattle and cane.
Slaves,
Naked and filthy,
Sold to the Grange Plantation
In Jamaica.
Hungry and weak,
Sold to the St. Lucia Plantation
In Cuba.
Sick and diseased,
Sold to the Charlack Plantation
In Carolina.

"Musafa,
Sold.
See him no more.
Hear him no more.
Shum Da Da We Da Shum Da Da We Da."

So saddened by what she had to report,
Water melted into the river,
Where her tears flooded the shore.

Wind's Chance

"*I am ready to go,*"
Said Wind.
"But you are not strong enough
To cross the Great Water,"
Dinga responded.
Wind wanted to argue,
But she knew he was right.
She swooshed away
To ponder the situation.

Now Dinga realized he was never going to see his son again.
Never stand beside him at the forge.
Devastated by the unfinished way they had been separated,
Dinga wept as he worked—
Clank! Clank! Clink! Clank! Clank! Clink!—
And then could work no more.
In grief,
Dinga let his fire go out.
Ore lay neglected.
His hammer, unused, rusted.
His bellows rotted.
Weeds grew around his anvil.

The rainy season came,
Followed by the dry season.
Another year—three now since Musafa had been taken.
On the hottest day
Wind came to Dinga and hovered over his head.

"I think I have found a way
To cross the Big Water
To search for our son.
My sisters will help me!"

Immediately, Wind began the long trip.
Just a wisp of air at first,
She started over Mother Earth's great desert,
The Sahara.
Gathering speed and heat,
Whipping up sand,
Wind let Fire throw lightning into the mix,
And she grew stronger.
Wind sucked up Water from the Atlantic,
And built more speed,
Spinning, twisting,
Changing, driving.
By the time she reached the Americas
With the help of her sisters,
She had been transformed into
Hurricane.

Months later,
Wind rode home to the Sahel
On the back of a high-flying cloud
Just in time for the rainy season,
Bringing new life to the grasslands.
Gentle as before, Wind
Curled herself around the blacksmith's neck.
"What word of my son do you bring?" he asked.
And this is the story she told.

Wind's Saga

"IBO, SONINKE, BENIN,
  Yoruba, Wolof, Akan, and Mandingo . . .
  All taken;
  All living in the Americas.
  I saw the Taken shackled
  To the land from sunup to sundown,
  Working tobacco, sugarcane, cotton, and rice fields.
  I visited the grand houses that their hands helped build.
  I listened to them sing and tell stories—
  Different,
  But strangely familiar.
  Characters I knew by other names:
  Anansi,
  Now Aunt Nancy;
  Zomo the Rabbit,
  Now Br'er Rabbit.
  I stopped by kitchens and watched our women
  Cook yams and okra,
  Rice and beans.
  Then I realized they had not forgotten.
  And I rejoiced.
  Led by the sound of a blacksmith's hammer,
  I traveled
  To Charleston, South Carolina.
  To a simple shop with a shingle—
John Shannon, Blacksmith.

JOHN
SHANNON

BLACKSMITH

"A large European with red hair and beard
Stood at the forge,
Comfortable among his tools—
Tongs, fullers, swages, hardies.
There were apprentices—all Africans—
Working on pieces,
Both new and old at the same time—
Familiar yet fresh.
Then Blacksmith Shannon said,
'Moses, I have sold another
Of your beautiful gates
In the wild rice design.
How did you learn to craft so well?'
A young man stepped into the light.
'I learn by reaching back with one hand
And stretching forward with the other,' he said.
'People say you are a genius!'
Said Blacksmith Shannon.
'My father, Dinga, was the genius,'
Replied the apprentice.
'He taught me what seven generations had learned.
I am the eighth.'

RECOGNITION

"I HAD FOUND Musafa,
   Our Musafa,
   Who answers now to Moses Shannon.
   Musafa . . . Moses—which means
   'Saved through the water.'
   He seems more confident at the forge now.
   Wiser.
   Yet I also saw in his eyes the playful Musafa
   We remember.
   I had so much to tell him;
   But he could not see me
   In this strange land.
   Nor could I make him hear me.
   Still, I kissed his brow.
   He touched the spot and smiled,
   As if remembering.

"Our son has truly found the music in his hammer.
   His fences, railings, and banisters
   Are handsomely decorated with birds, flowers,
   And animals inspired by his memories of home.
   I heard someone tell Moses,
   'Blacksmith Shannon is going to free you
   One day soon.'
   And to my joy, I heard Musafa whisper,
   'In my mind I have always been free,
   As free as Wind.'
   Swi Swi a Swi Swi a Swi Swi a Swi Wa."

THE CELEBRATION

"My son, Musafa, is a blacksmith
In a land called Charleston!" Dinga cried.
"Though a slave, he lives!"
He shouted louder,
And ran to tell his neighbors.

"Who told you this, Blacksmith?"
"Why, Wind told me!"
(The villagers still talk about the day
Dinga the blacksmith went mad.)
Dinga rushed to the next house and the next.
"My son never forgot
What he learned at my forge!" he cried.
("Such a fantastic story; how can he expect us to believe him?")
Dinga hurried to the marketplace.
"My son is alive and well and for this I am grateful."
He clapped his hands,
Raised them over his head, and rejoiced.
("Dinga is mad, but he is happy in his madness, so let him be.")

Dinga danced and feasted far into the night
With the Mother Elements by his side,
Celebrating the son who was taken,
But never forgotten.

COMES THE SILENCE

Today.
Mali, West Africa.

The last part of a story is the silence
That comes at the end.
A time to think, to reflect.
The drums are still now.
They no longer warn us
To beware
Of the men who steal upriver. . . .
Countless numbers are gone forever, stolen.
Griots still tell
Of Musafa,
Who was but one of millions captured;
Of Dinga,
Who was but one of many fathers who mourned.
Loved ones are never forgotten
When we continue to tell their stories.

What father can hide his pain
When his child is stolen?
What mother does not lament
The loss of a son or daughter?
Remember the wisdom of Mother Dongi:
"Kings may come and go,
But the family endures forever."
Think on that when the silence comes.

Author's Note

For years I have been curious about how African literature and music portray those who were captured in the slave trade. I am certain that African mothers cried for their lost children, their brothers and sisters, their neighbors and friends. But I could not find any lyrics that a grieving parent might have sung. Where were the stories—told and retold—so the lost ones would never be forgotten? Where were the rituals or ceremonies that showed how Africans mourned the Taken? Where were the dances, annual feasts, and fasting days? None found. Yet certainly the captured were loved and missed.

I wanted to write about the lost ones. And so I turned to African history and folktales.

After studying the slave trade, I discovered that Mende blacksmiths were honored and respected for their seemingly magical skills at the forge. They were said to have commanded the four elements—Earth, Fire, Water, and Wind. In the Americas, African blacksmiths combined their skills with those of European smiths and created a unique style easily recognized in places like New Orleans, Charleston, and Savannah.

Later, when I visited the Caribbean island of Barbados, I heard a wonderful legend that described the nature of hurricanes. It was said that a hurricane was Mother Africa in search of her lost children.

Using these various elements, I have tried to create a story that addresses the question all of us who are descendants of the Taken ask: "Were we missed?" I answer with a resounding "Yes! We were *never forgotten*."

Patricia C. McKissack
Chesterfield, Missouri